Yummy Yuk!

First published in Great Britain 1990 by Heinemann Young Books
an imprint of Reed International Books Limited.
Michelin House, 81 Fulham Rd, London SW3 6RB
Mammoth paperback edition first published 1998
Published in hardback by Heinemann Educational Publishers,
a division of Reed Educational and Professional Publishing Limited
by arrangement with Reed International Books Limited.
Text copyright © Heather Maisner 1990
Illustrations copyright © Alicia Garcia de Lynam 1990
The Author and Illustrator have asserted their moral rights
Paperback ISBN 0 7497 3539 2
Hardback ISBN 0 434 80376 6
10 9 8 7 6 5 4 3 2 1
A CIP catalogue record for this title is available from the British Library
Printed at Oriental Press Limited, Dubai

Heather Maisner

Yummy Yuk!

Illustrated by
Alicia Garcia de Lynam

 **YELLOW BANANAS**

For Ali B and Georgia May

Chapter One
A Cold Dark Alley

SONNY AND SLIM played football on the village dump. They'd set up a goal using their jackets to mark the goal posts, and over and over they kicked and caught and caught and kicked the ball. Then Sonny kicked harder than ever before. The ball spun through the air and landed in Poison Row, where it bounced down the alley.

'Now look what you've
done,' said Slim.

'You should've caught it,' said
Sonny.

'You kicked it too high.'

'You should've jumped higher.'

The boys frowned at each other.

'Now what?'

'I'll get it,' said Slim, and before Sonny
could stop him, he ran off.

'Don't,' cried Sonny. 'Don't go there, you
dummy.' But Slim ignored him. He just kept
on running.

No one ever went down Poison Row. No
one lived there, except Oz Poison, known as
Poz. And no one ever wanted to meet Poz.

It was cold and dark down Poison Row and

the alley was covered in a damp mist. The empty houses had broken windows and they looked like broken teeth on ugly faces. Shutters banged, doors clattered and handles rattled.

Slim shivered. He wanted to turn round and run back to his friend, but the echoing bounce of the ball led him down the narrow lane like a magnet.

On and on he ran, until suddenly a hand reached out and grabbed his shoulder. It was old and hard and knobbly. He screamed.

There was a dreadful smell, an ugly shape, bright eyes and broken teeth.

'Looking for this?' asked a terrible voice.

Slim looked up and nodded, too frightened to speak.

'I'll give you back your ball,' said Poz, 'but I've got a job for you to do first.'

He yanked Slim through a large black door in the wall.

Chapter Two
Come Back!

'SLIM, SLIM, COME back.'

Sonny stood at the entrance to Poison Row and called his friend's name over and over.

He waited as the sun went down, then slowly he began to walk down the dark alley. But the clanging shutters and the banging doors terrified him, and he soon ran back again. For everyone knew that anyone who went down Poison Row was never heard of again.

Chapter Three
Yummy Yuk

'THIS WAY,' GROWLED Poz. 'Don't you want your ball?'

Slim dragged his feet and said nothing. All he wanted was to get away.

They were in an underground passage. It was dark and smelly, just as everyone said Poz's home was. They also said Poz ate pigs' ears, red ants and slugs. His skin was like a crocodile's. His hair was as spiky as a

hedgehog's. His teeth were sharp as a tiger's. And when he spoke he growled like a dog. These people were right.

The corridor was wet and slippery. The smell was like bad eggs topped with icing sugar. The noise was like a vacuum cleaner tied to a pin-ball machine worked by robots.

Suddenly Poz pulled Slim through a doorway into an enormous hall with an arched ceiling, a balcony and a glass office in the centre. Down on the floor stood row after row of machines, clanking and whining and

tapping and bleeping. The stench in the room
was revolting.

'Do you like eating?' Poz shouted above the
noise.

Slim didn't answer. Was Poz going to make
him eat pigs' ears and slugs and revolting red
ants that would choke him and sting him as
he swallowed them down?

'Over here,' said Poz, and he dragged
Slim to a large cauldron in the middle of
the room where two chutes carried
brown and green goo from the
machines.

Poz lowered a ladle into the
cauldron and raised it
slowly.

The goo slurped off in dollops, then
squelched into a bowl.

'Now,' said Poz, 'how about a little
taste?'

Slim gulped. 'I can't,' he mumbled.

'Speak up, boy,' said Poz.

'I said I can't eat it.'

'Of course you can. Boys are always
hungry.'

'Well I'm not,' said Slim. 'Anyway I can't eat this. It looks like muck and it stinks.'

'Well, what should it look like? What colour should it be?'

'Pink,' said Slim, off the top of his head. 'And fruity . . . like candy floss and raspberry ripple and er . . . er . . . strawberry whip.'

'I see.'

Poz pressed a button. A machine squirted pink gloss over Slim's bowl.

'It still stinks,' said Slim.

Poz pressed another button and a spray of rosy perfume wafted over Slim's bowl.

'Eat!' Poz barked.

'It's gooey and yukky and horrible,' said Slim. 'I can't.'

'If you want your ball back, eat!'

Slim held his nose and took a tiny lick. 'Yuk,' he said.

'One more taste,' barked Poz. 'And you can go.'

Slim brought the spoon to his mouth, held his breath, closed his eyes and swallowed a

whole mouthful of the green and pink goo.
As it touched his lips, he frowned. As it
swirled around his mouth, he grimaced. As it
slithered down his throat, he gulped. Then his
face relaxed and he let out a sigh. He opened
his eyes and stared at Poz.

'Well?' asked Poz.

'Well,' said Slim. 'Yuk. I mean yummy
yummy yuk. Can I have some more?'

Poz's face creased into a smile. For years

he'd been working to produce a food that
children would love, a food that would make
him his fortune. At last he had found it –
sweet and salty, sticky and slimy, not too firm
but firm enough, not too real yet real enough.
It was perfect. His lizard's eyes blinked as
Slim ate it all up.

'More,' said Slim. 'Can I have some more?'

It was as delicious as chocolate or ice-
cream. More desirable than crisps or sweets.
More wonderful than anything he'd ever eaten
before. The more he ate the more he wanted.

'Enough,' barked Poz.

'But I want some more!' said Slim.

'Not now!' snapped Poz. 'Watch out for me at the supermarket next week.'

He dragged Slim down the corridor to the black door and flung the ball down the alley. He pushed Slim out after it and slammed the door shut. Slim stood uncertainly by the door, then walked slowly down the misty street.

Chapter Four
Something's Different

WHEN SONNY SAW the ball bounce out of
Poison Row, he knew his friend was safe.
And when at last Slim appeared, Sonny ran to
greet him.

'Thank goodness you're back,' he said.

'Yeah,' said Slim, but he didn't look very
pleased.

'And you found the ball. Fantastic.' Sonny
dribbled it across the dump. 'I thought I'd
never see you again,' he laughed.

Sonny kicked the ball towards Slim, but
Slim didn't dive towards it or even chase after
it. He simply hung back at the entrance to
Poison Row.

'You all right?' asked Sonny.

'Yeah,' said Slim. 'Except I'm starving.'

'So am I,' said Sonny. 'Race you to the fish
and chip shop. Come on.'

'But I don't want fish and chips,' said Slim.
'I want Yummy Yuk.'

'What's that?' asked Sonny. 'I've never heard of it.'

'It's what Poz gave me.'

'You mean you met him? You met him and ate his food?'

'Yeah,' said Slim. 'That's how I got the ball back.'

'You should have left the ball there,' said Sonny.

'Well I didn't, did I? And do you know what? I liked his food. It's the best food I ever ate.'

'But you don't know what's in it. People say . . .'

'I know what people say, but I've eaten it and I love it. And next week Poz is going to bring it to the supermarket.'

Slim ran off, singing 'Yummy Yuk, Yummy Yuk, Yummy Yuk.'

Sonny felt numb. Something had happened to Slim, though he didn't know what. He picked up the ball and, cuddling it against him, he walked slowly home.

Chapter Five
An Evil Man

AT SUPPER SONNY asked his parents about
Oz Poison.

'You haven't been playing down Poison
Row, have you?' his mother said quickly.

'No, Mum,' said Sonny. 'The ball went down
there, that's all. But who is he?'

'He's an evil man,' Sonny's father replied. 'A
scientist who uses science for his own ends.'

'But what did he do?' Sonny asked.

'First he created a soap powder that made your clothes clean but, when you put them on, your skin itched and burned. Then he created a shampoo that was supposed to be ideal for all types of hair. In fact it made everyone's hair fall out.'

'And the toothpaste he produced ruined people's gums,' continued his mother. 'He wanted to make money and he didn't care how he did it. Eventually, he was chased into hiding but he swore he'd be back.'

'If he made some food, would it be bad?' Sonny asked.

'It certainly would,' his father replied. 'Everything he does is bad, so keep away from Poz and Poison Row.'

Sonny felt a shiver creep down his back.

Chapter Six
Poz Hits Town

THE FOLLOWING WEDNESDAY, Oz Poison made his first appearance in town for over twenty years.

Dressed in a green suit and tie, he strode out of Poison Row. His skin shone like polished leather, his spiky hair glistened and his lizard's eyes blinked. In his arms he cradled some cans.

When the people of the town saw him, they stopped what they were doing and followed him.

Outside the supermarket Slim was waiting and Sonny was arguing with him. Slim's eyes were wild. He hadn't eaten for days. The only food he wanted was Yummy Yuk.

'Come on, Slim. Let's play football,' said Sonny.

'I can't. I'm waiting,' said Slim.

'For what?'

'For him, you dummy.'

'But he isn't coming,' said Sonny.

'He will,' Slim insisted.

And at that moment Poz turned the corner, strode into the supermarket and demanded to see the manager.

'I told you,' said Slim. 'I knew he'd come.'

Mr Boss, the supermarket manager, liked neatness and order. He liked shelves stacked with equal-sized cans, packets with matching labels and the aisles clear. He didn't like people crowding into the doorway, as they were at this moment, nor did he like the strange fellow who was waiting for him.

'What can I do for you, Sir?' Mr Boss demanded.

'Nothing,' said Poz. 'I'm going to do something for you. I'm going to give you the privilege of stocking the first-ever can of the most amazing food that has ever been created, food that children everywhere have been waiting for, food that the world has wanted for centuries.' With a flourish

he held up the first packaged and labelled
can of Yummy Yuk.

The crowd craned forward to see.

'I'm sorry,' said Mr Boss. 'Our shelves are
completely full.'

'Rubbish,' said Poz. 'You'll find room for this.'

'Also,' Mr Boss continued, 'new products are first tested by our team of experts and I have

to say that I doubt whether anything wrapped in a bright green label and called Yummy Yuk will sell.'

'It will,' snapped Poz. 'How can you turn this away without even trying it? Or do you wish to be remembered as the man who refused to taste the most desirable food of all time?'

'Well . . .' Mr Boss hesitated.

Poz opened the can and a rich, dark smell filled the store. The crowd held their noses and stepped back.

'It smells rather strong,' said Mr Boss.

'So do game and caviar and truffles, but they're good, aren't they? Try some,' said Poz, pushing the can closer to Mr Boss.

'Oh very well,' Mr Boss grimaced as Poz handed him a spoonful of Yuk. He took a quick lick and backed away. 'In my considered opinion this food is not right for our store,' he said. 'And if I don't like it I'm sure no child will.'

'But I do,' cried Slim. 'Give it to me.'

He squeezed through the crowd, snatched the spoon out of Mr Boss's hand, and licked it clean.

'Well I never.' Mr Boss was amazed.

'I told you children love it,' said Poz, scooping up another spoonful for the manager.

'Yuk,' said Mr Boss, as he swallowed it down. 'It's really rather yummy.'

'More,' said Slim, reaching out for the can, but Mr Boss took it first.

'Fill some shelves with Yummy Yuk,' he called to his staff. 'This way please Mr . . . er . . . Mr . . . er . . .'

'Poison,' said Poz, and he followed Mr Boss into his office.

Chapter Seven

Special Offer!

MR BOSS PUT Yummy Yuk on special offer so that it cost less than any other food in the store. Slim bought one can after another, and every child who saw him eating bought some Yummy Yuk. By evening all the cans had been sold.

The next day the staff filled more shelves with Yummy Yuk.

'There it is. There's Yummy Yuk,' the children said as they strolled down the aisles. By evening all the cans had been sold.

On the third day the staff filled even more shelves with Yuk.

'We want it. We want it,' the children cried, and by evening all these cans had been sold.

On the fourth day the staff filled all the shelves with Yummy Yuk.

'Give us Yuk. Give us Yuk. Give us Yummy Yummy Yuk!' the children screamed.

Days and nights passed and the children became more and more greedy. They didn't

laugh. They didn't smile. They didn't talk or sing, or wash or change their clothes. They grew fatter and fatter and their skin began to turn green just like the Yuk they were eating.

They didn't want chocolate or crisps any more and the ice-cream van no longer came to town. And every day as soon as the supermarket doors opened, children crowded

in. Scratching and biting, screaming and fighting, they opened the cans and poured Yuk into their mouths. They spilt it on their clothes, threw it at the walls, dropped it on the floor and skated in it.

And still they cried:

'Give us Yuk. Give us Yuk. Give us Yummy Yummy Yuk.'

The parents gathered outside the store and began to question the food their children were eating:

'What is this Yuk?' Slim's mother asked.

'The label should tell us,' said one boy's father.

But the label didn't list the ingredients so they called for the manager. When Mr Boss arrived, looking green in the face, he simply said:

'We stock what children like. Surely you can see how much your children like what we stock?'

Nobody knew what to do.

Chapter Eight
HELP!

SOON SONNY WAS the only boy in town
who refused to eat Yuk. One day he pushed
his way through the noisy children to Slim.

'Let's play football,' he said, bouncing the
ball. 'Like we used to.'

'I'm eating,' said Slim. 'Can't you see?'

When Slim had swallowed the last
mouthful, Sonny said:

'Let's go.'

But Slim seemed not to hear him.

'I think I'll have some more Yuk,' he said.

'Don't,' said Sonny. 'Please, don't.'

'Is he causing trouble?' Oliver Fatso asked, forcing his enormous bulk between the two boys.

'Well . . .' Slim hesitated. 'Yeah, he wants me to play football. Imagine playing football.'

'What you need is something nice to eat.' Fatso said, holding Sonny's arm. 'Why don't you try some Yuk?'

'Because it's revolting,' said Sonny.

'Are you saying what I eat is revolting?'

'Yes. Yuk stinks and so do all of you.'

And it was true. Standing among them was like standing in a field of manure.

'He said we stink,' shouted Fatso. 'Get him.'

Sonny pulled his arm away but Fatso stuck out his foot and Sonny fell.

'Give him some Yuk,' he shouted, pushing a can of green and pink goo in front of his nose.

'No!' screamed Sonny. 'No!'

He kicked the can away and tried to escape. But children surrounded him, aiming dollops of Yuk at him. Sonny leapt over their fat bodies and darted between their legs to the door. Behind him, one by one, the children stumbled to the floor and began to lick up the Yuk they'd been throwing.

Only Slim remained standing.

'Wait, Sonny. Wait,' he said.

He lifted his foot to kick the football to Sonny, but he couldn't. His heavy body slumped down into a pool of Yuk.

'Help me, Sonny. Help us all,' he cried. 'You're the only one who can.'

Sonny ran home. He flung himself down on his bed and cried and cried because he was lonely and because his friends were in trouble and he didn't know how to help them. Then slowly a plan formed in his mind. He picked up a pen and began to write a letter.

Chapter Nine
Sonny's Plan

THE FOLLOWING WEDNESDAY at 4 o'clock
Mr Tester, the health inspector, arrived in
town. Mothers, fathers, aunts, uncles and
grandparents followed him to the
supermarket.

'I understand that Yummy Yuk does not list
its ingredients and could be harmful to
children's health,' the inspector told Mr Boss.

'Nonsense,' growled Mr Boss. 'It's what
children want.'

'Give us Yuk. Give us Yuk. Give us Yummy Yummy Yuk,' the children chorused around him.

'But I'm a child and I don't want it,' said Sonny springing in front of the inspector. 'And I'm the only boy in town who can still run and jump and play football.'

'That's true,' said the parents. 'Yuk has made our children fat and ugly and bad tempered.'

Mr Tester looked from the screaming children to Sonny and back again.

'I'm afraid I must remove these cans for testing,' he said.

'No,' cried a terrible voice from the back of the store. 'Don't touch those cans. Nobody will have my secret.' Poz pushed his way through the crowd. 'Yuk can do no harm. I'll show you.'

Everybody stood still and watched, as roaring and shouting, Poz snatched up can after can of Yummy Yuk and poured the mixture straight into his mouth. His body

grew large and heavy. His face became
swollen and fat. His skin turned dark, dark
green. Finally he picked up the last can and
drank down the very last of the green and
pink mixture. He closed his eyes, leant back
against the shelves and repeated over and
over:

'Yummy Yuk. Yummy Yuk. Yummy Yummy . . .' Then he let out a long shrill 'Yuk' and exploded with a gigantic

POP!

A horrible smell filled the store.
On the floor where Poz had stood was a
thick mud-green puddle. Slowly it rolled
down the aisles, through the doors, across
the pavement, along the kerb and slurped
down the drain.

That was the last anyone ever saw of Oz Poison (though some still say he's in hiding down Poison Row) and the last time anyone ever bought a can of Poz's Yummy Yuk.

Everything is fine in the town now. The children are happy and healthy again and every day after school Sonny and Slim play football on the dump once more. At the end of the game they race to the supermarket to buy fruit and drinks and tasty snacks. And Mr Boss, in a neat shirt and tie, rings up the till with a smile.

Yellow Bananas are bright, funny, brilliantly imaginative stories written by some of today's top writers. All the books are beautifully illustrated in full colour.

So if you've enjoyed this story, why not pick another one from the bunch?